For my children, Ottilie, Rufus and Agatha

BLOOMSBURY CHILDREN'S BOOKS
Bloomsbury Publishing Plc
50 Bedford Square, London WC1B 3DP, UK

BLOOMSBURY, BLOOMSBURY CHILDREN'S BOOKS and the Diana logo are trademarks of Bloomsbury Publishing Plc

First published in Great Britain in January 2021 by Bloomsbury Publishing Plc

First published in the USA in October 2020 by Bloomsbury Children's Books
1385 Broadway, New York, New York 10018

A catalogue record for this book is available from the British Library

ISBN 978 1 5266 3112 1 (HB)
ISBN 978 1 5266 3111 4 (eBook)

2 4 6 8 10 9 7 5 3 1

Printed in China by Leo Paper Products, Heshan, Guangdong

All papers used by Bloomsbury Publishing Plc are natural, recyclable products from wood grown in well-managed forests.
The manufacturing processes conform to the environmental regulations of the country of origin

To find out more about our authors and books visit www.bloomsbury.com and sign up for our newsletters

The Song for Everyone

Lucy Morris

BLOOMSBURY
CHILDREN'S BOOKS
LONDON OXFORD NEW YORK NEW DELHI SYDNEY

It was just a tiny window, too **high** in the eaves to be noticed from below and too small to let in much daylight.

And yet one morning out came a delicate tune.

A melody,

a song,

a sound so sweet

drifted out on to the breeze and down into the lanes below.

The schoolboy had a long and lonely walk each morning.

As he passed beneath the small window
he stopped to listen to the music.

His loneliness instantly forgotten, he
felt as **light** as a feather. The music
and the delighted boy

                       bounced

                            away

                                together.

Nearby, the old lady hobbled slowly to town for bread and milk.
She felt the **chill** of the breeze in her aching bones.

As she walked, a trickle of notes tickled her ears. She rested
for a moment beneath the little window and **listened**.

The sound flowed down and **wrapped** itself around her weary body.

At that moment she felt so lively

and **full of joy**.

Tired and hungry, the cat from nowhere in particular took a nap in the afternoon sun.

Her ears **pricked** up at the delicate sound.

The music seemed to be whispering, *"Little cat, little cat, follow me."*

Notes dangled just out of reach and led her to the children
from Rose Lane who **longed** for a cat of their very own.

Over time it seemed that the music gave the
townspeople something they had been **missing**.

It searched out the lonely and lost, the needy and sad.

And above all, it made the people of the town care for one another. They shared food and stories and kindnesses.

The days passed in peace and contentment.

Until one morning, without warning, the window was

completely

and utterly

silent.

All the townspeople woke feeling exhausted and grumpy.

The bread wouldn't rise, the milkman arrived late,
and the café owner simply stayed in bed.

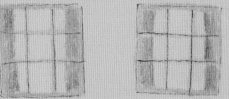

DOLLY'S BAKERY

THE
LITTLE
CAFE

closed

closed

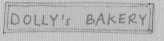

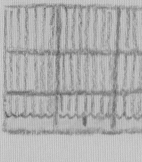

Even the flowers drooped in their window boxes.

Why had the magical music stopped? What was to be
done? A **meeting** was called and the matter discussed.

The lonely schoolboy felt brave enough
to climb up to the little window. Eventually
he reached the wonky ledge and hopped inside.

There in the dusty corner lay a tiny wren.
She opened her beak but no sound escaped.

"It was just you singing for us?" he asked. "You must be so tired."

"I will help you," the boy whispered, and the little bird blinked back
as though she understood every word.

The boy shouted down to the people below.

And everyone knew just what to do.

Two long days passed without a sound from
the little window. The townspeople anxiously
awaited even the slightest hint of a tune.

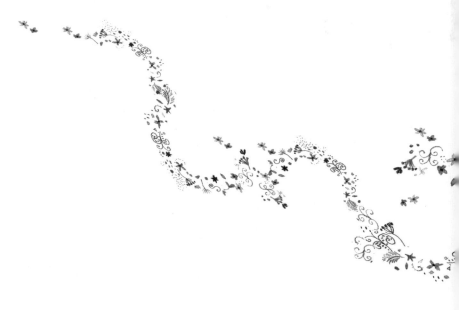

Oh, what joy!

A melody. A song. A sound so sweet.

It drifted out on to the breeze and down into the lanes below,
growing louder and more joyful with each beautiful note.

Everyone leaped from their beds and flew into the street,
not quite believing their ears. There in the little window
stood the boy and the wren making music together.

Singing the song for everyone.

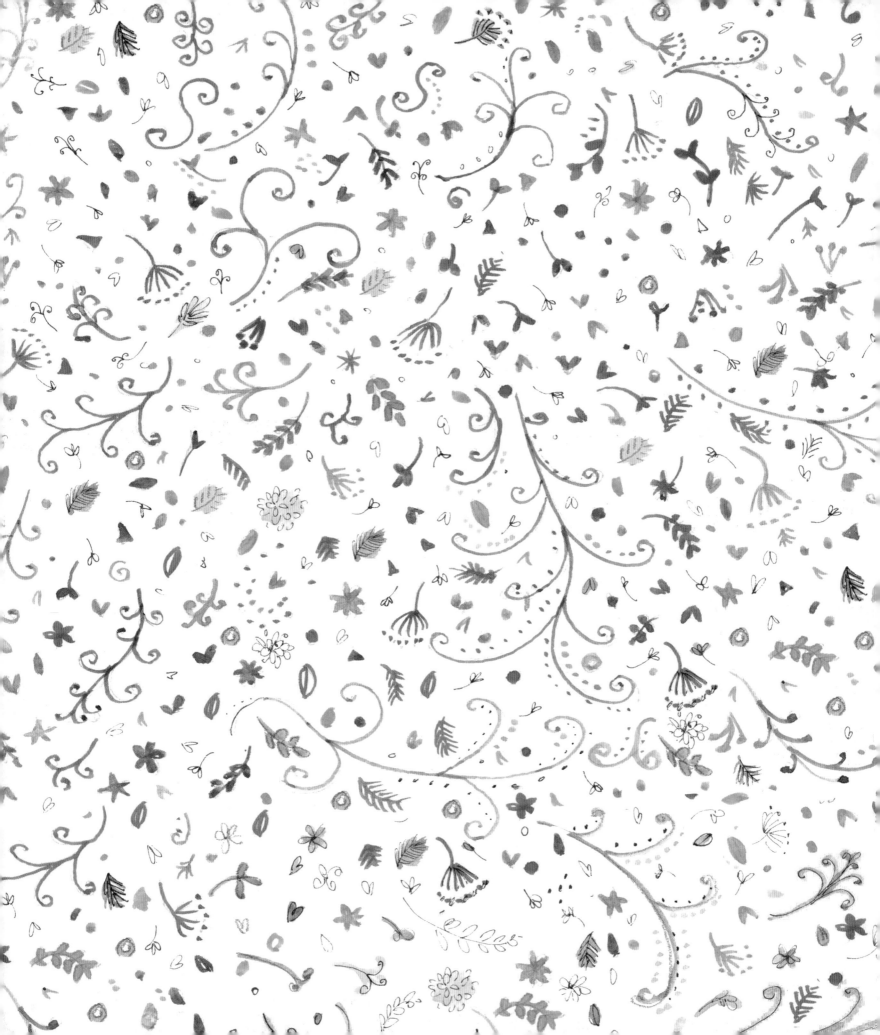